To Edith & Eliza,

May life's adventures challenge you, guide you & bring you tremendous joy & love.

When life gets tough, look for the beauty in the darkest corners & the brightest places. It will be there when you look hard enough.

Paul H.

FINDING
ELIZABETH BEAUTY

2003

Elizabeth Sees the World
Finding Beauty

PAUL L SHIPTON

In the middle of the Britannical Sea lies the small
island of Angelplot.
And if ever you should wander across its
green fields and rolling hills,
You may find yourself among the ruins of a grand old
castle atop the northern mountains.

This is no ordinary castle. Back in the tenth century,
Northtop Castle was world famous, for it was
the home of the rulers of Angelplot.

The rulers of Angelplot were not only
powerful, but also learned, wise, and magical.
It was said they could heal the
ills of their people with a snap of their
fingers or the wink of an eye.

One of the most powerful rulers
to ever sit on the throne was Old Man
Mellow, a ruler so learned and powerful
that he could bring people back from the
very brink of death.

Old Man Mellow came from a long line of revered rulers, a responsibility and honor that would one day be adopted by his only child, the Princess Elizabeth.

As he grew older, and nearer to his own death, he became concerned about Elizabeth.

Elizabeth had great potential. She was powerful and destined for greatness. But when she was younger, she was also a little reckless. Her curiosity would often land her in trouble. She had much to learn before taking over from her father.

Where they lived, everything was beautiful.
The castle with its soaring towers,
The forest with its majestic trees,
And the hills with their gentle ups and downs.

Elizabeth had never known anything other than the beauty that
surrounded her, and so assumed the outside world would be just the same.

"The ruler of Angelplot can only be fully ready when they have been out into the world. It is time to put your curiosity to the test!" said her father. "It is time for you to see the world for what it is."

"Is it not just like this?" asked Elizabeth. "Is it not beautiful?" "Of course it is," replied Mellow. "But beauty is complicated, and so is the outside world. Pretty things aren't always as pretty as they seem. Even a beautiful rose has its thorns."

He went on, "I'm sending you to see Prince Méchant. You will have to travel over the ocean to Jelait. He will give you a gift. The final thing you need to ready yourself as ruler."

With excitement, her curiosity piqued, she packed her bag, and went off, out into the world.

She walked many miles that first day.
At dusk, she came across the most
beautiful river.
She put her hand in, feeling the cool blue
water flow between her fingers. Tiny fish
danced under the surface and flowers
bloomed along the bank.

"A beautiful place to spend my first night," she thought to herself. She drifted off to sleep with the sweet sound of trickling water in her ears.

Thunder woke her suddenly in the dead of night. A storm was raging. As she looked around her, she could see that the overflowing river had turned angry and had washed away all of her possessions.

She ran for help.

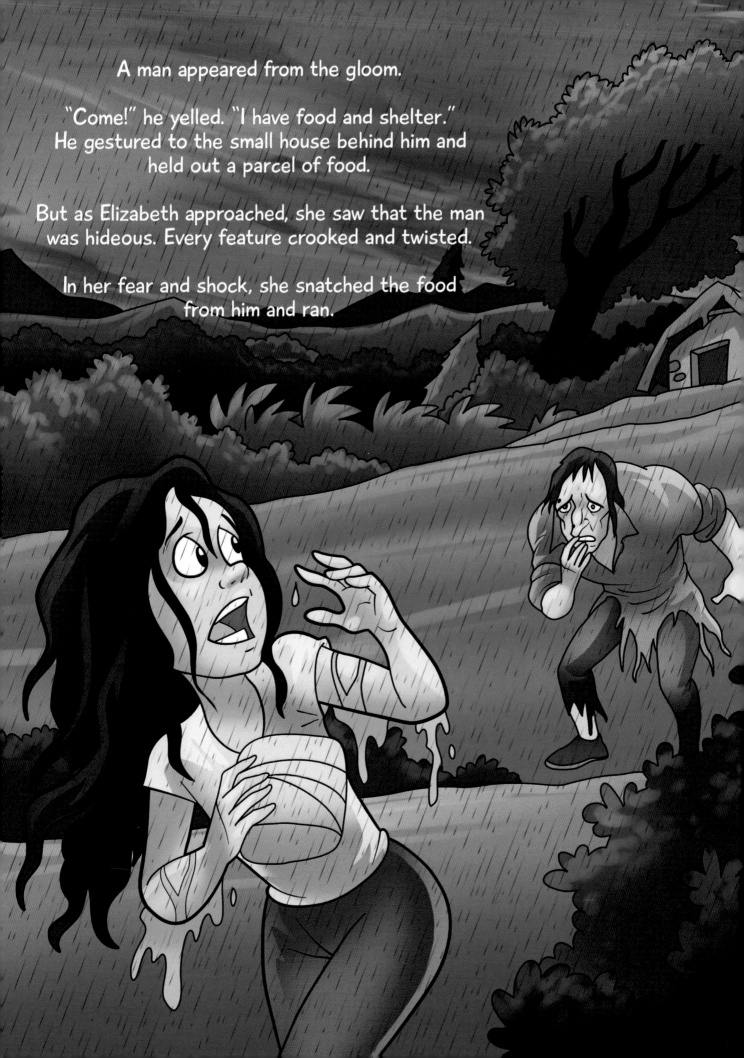

A man appeared from the gloom.

"Come!" he yelled. "I have food and shelter."
He gestured to the small house behind him and
held out a parcel of food.

But as Elizabeth approached, she saw that the man
was hideous. Every feature crooked and twisted.

In her fear and shock, she snatched the food
from him and ran.

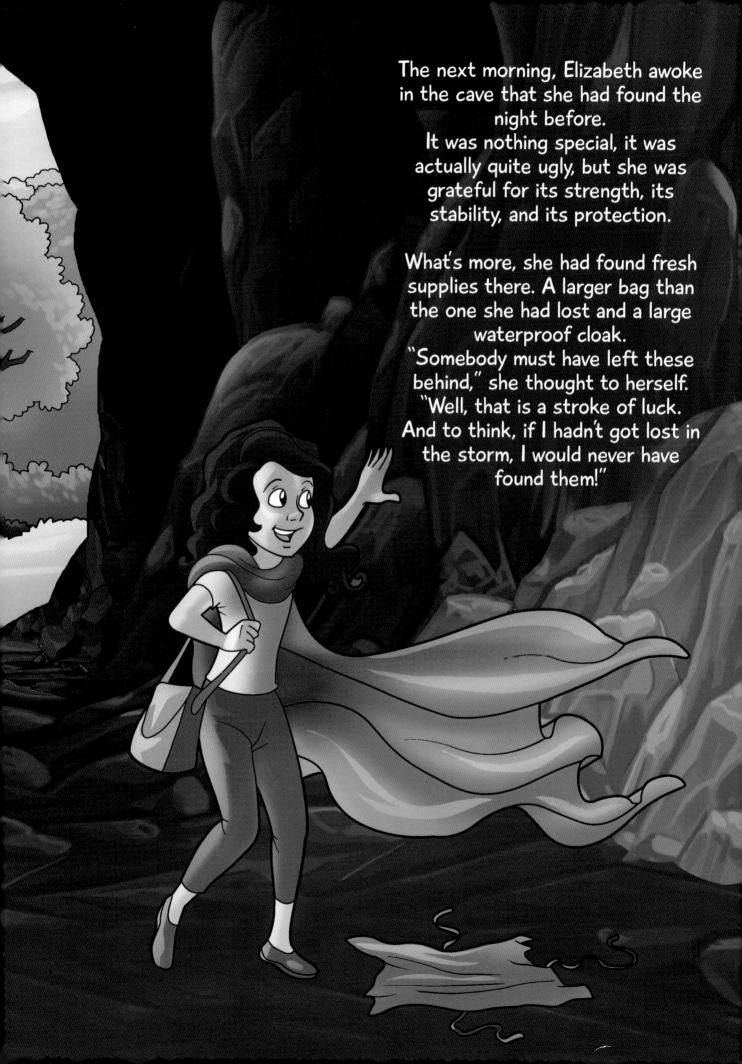

The next morning, Elizabeth awoke in the cave that she had found the night before.
It was nothing special, it was actually quite ugly, but she was grateful for its strength, its stability, and its protection.

What's more, she had found fresh supplies there. A larger bag than the one she had lost and a large waterproof cloak.
"Somebody must have left these behind," she thought to herself.
"Well, that is a stroke of luck. And to think, if I hadn't got lost in the storm, I would never have found them!"

That day, she managed to make it to the ocean, where a boat was waiting for her. It was worn and battered from years of sailing, and Elizabeth didn't much like the sight of it. But the journey was smooth and calm.

When traveling through Jelait, she stumbled across many a poor village. Each village was full of families living in squalor. They sheltered in small, run-down huts, had little to eat, and were filthy.

Still, they were happy. Happy and generous. Each village would share what little they had with Elizabeth. Their food, their water, their shelter, their stories. They may not have been beautiful to look at, yet their beautiful spirit shone brighter than any diamond.

The villagers taught Elizabeth a lot about seeing the brighter side of things.
In one village, an old lady told her a story. "I've been happily married to my husband for many years now. And you know, it's all because I missed a boat I was supposed to be on. If I hadn't missed that boat, I wouldn't have met him."

In another village, Elizabeth was talking to a young blacksmith. "I've always wanted to be a blacksmith, you see. It just so happened that my boss, Mr. Clink, was looking for a new apprentice just as I lost my job at the farm. He hardly ever takes on new apprentices, so I was very lucky. Now that's what I call a 'silver lining'!"

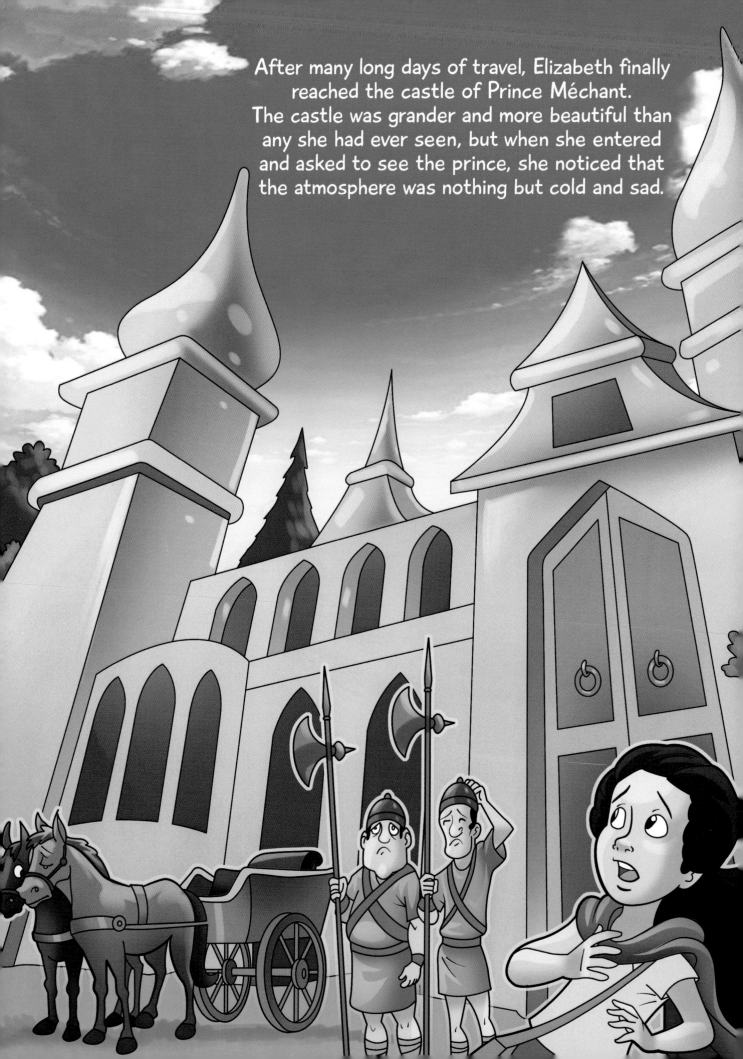

After many long days of travel, Elizabeth finally reached the castle of Prince Méchant. The castle was grander and more beautiful than any she had ever seen, but when she entered and asked to see the prince, she noticed that the atmosphere was nothing but cold and sad.

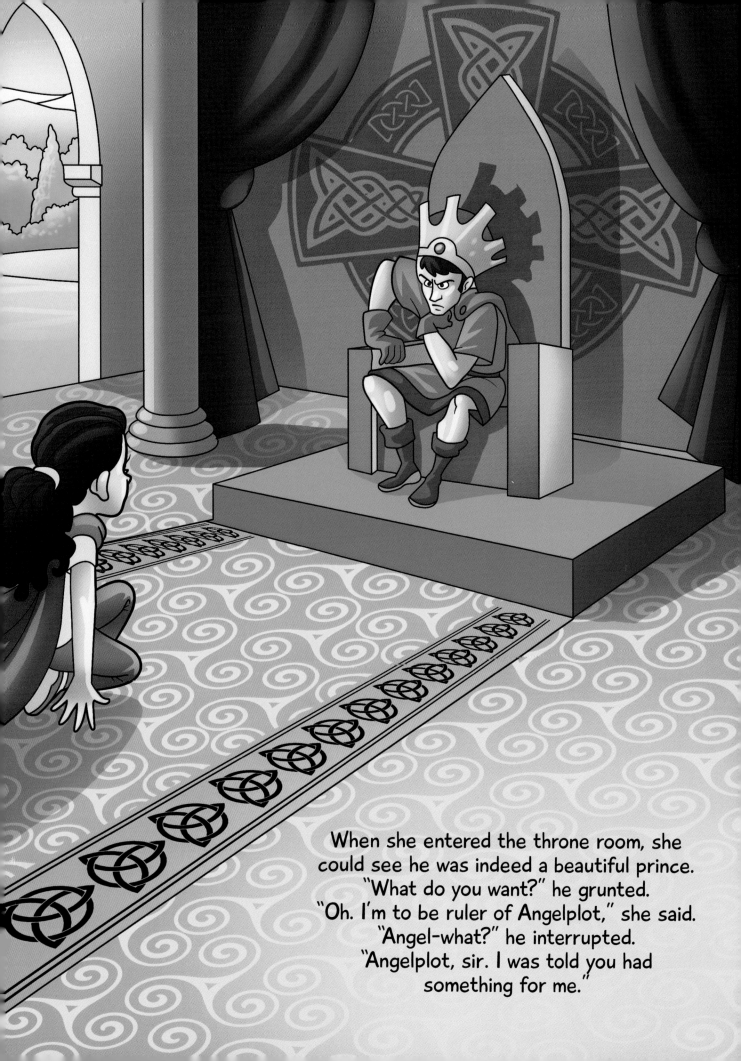

When she entered the throne room, she
could see he was indeed a beautiful prince.
"What do you want?" he grunted.
"Oh. I'm to be ruler of Angelplot," she said.
"Angel-what?" he interrupted.
"Angelplot, sir. I was told you had
something for me."

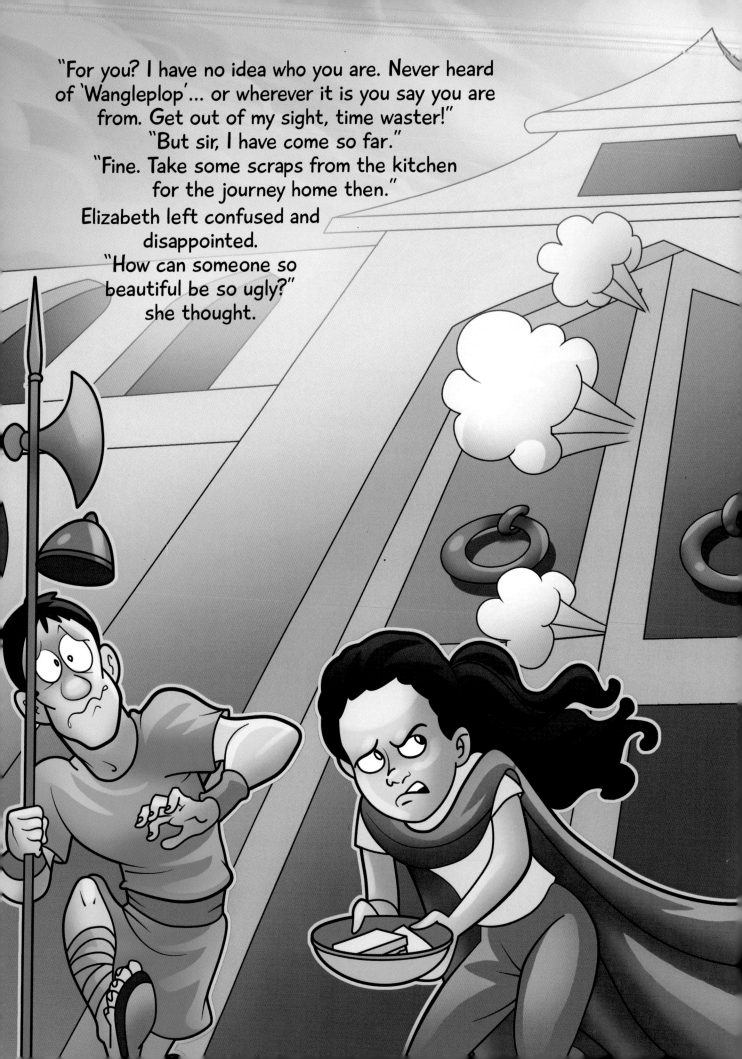

She thought deep and hard all the way home. After a while, she came across the ugly stranger from the night of the storm. He smiled and waved. And just like that, she understood.

She thought about all that she had seen...
The river, The cave, The villages.

She thought about all the people she had met... The villagers, The prince, This man in front of her. She thought about silver linings... How she had found that cloak and bag this man must have left her during the storm, How the old lady had met her husband, How the blacksmith had found his dream job.

Everything in the world had beauty, even if some of it was ugly as well. And even when things went wrong, often it led to other things going right!

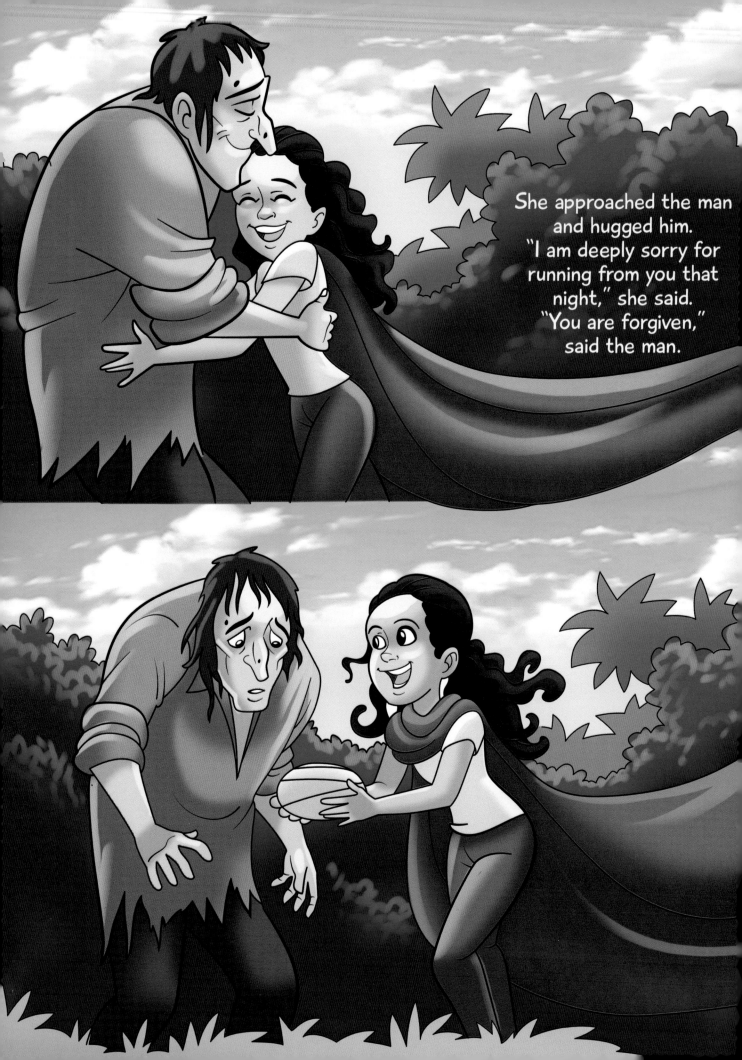

She approached the man and hugged him. "I am deeply sorry for running from you that night," she said. "You are forgiven," said the man.

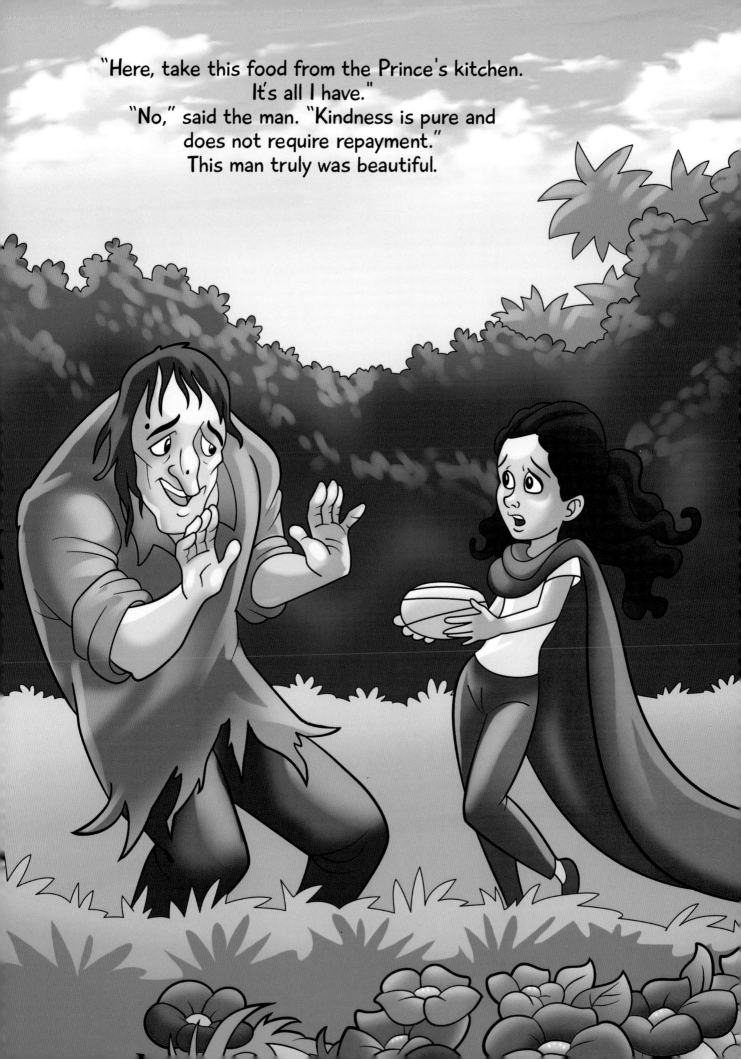

"Here, take this food from the Prince's kitchen.
It's all I have."
"No," said the man. "Kindness is pure and
does not require repayment."
This man truly was beautiful.

When she returned to Northtop Castle and hugged her father, he smiled and asked, "So... what did you see? What did you learn?"

"I saw beautiful things," she answered, "and terrible things..." Mellow nodded along wisely. "But I discovered that everything has beauty, you just have to look for it and focus on it. There is always a bright side," she finished.

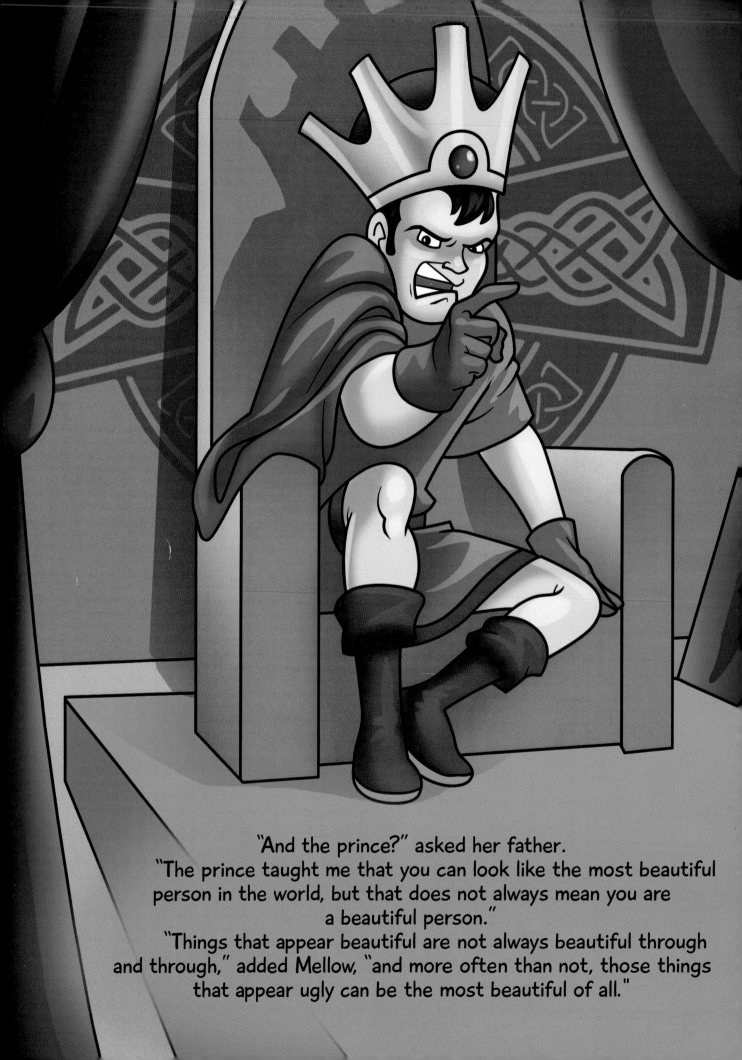

"And the prince?" asked her father.
"The prince taught me that you can look like the most beautiful
person in the world, but that does not always mean you are
a beautiful person."
"Things that appear beautiful are not always beautiful through
and through," added Mellow, "and more often than not, those things
that appear ugly can be the most beautiful of all."

After her journey, and her newfound wisdom, Old Man Mellow knew that his daughter was ready.
She became a ruler as wise and kind as her father, and perhaps the most famous ruler ever to sit on the throne of Angelplot at Northtop Castle.

THE END